First published in 1998
by Hodder Children's Books
a division of Hodder Headline Limited
338 Euston Road
London NW1 3BH

This edition published in 2000

Text copyright © 1998 John Cunliffe
Story copyright © 1998 Ivor Wood and John Cunliffe
Illustrations copyright © 1998 Hodder Children's Books
and Woodland Animations Ltd

ISBN 0 340 77344 8
10 9 8 7 6 5 4 3 2 1

A catalogue record for this book is available from the British Library.

Printed in Hong Kong

Four Stories in One

Postman Pat ™

Postman Pat and the surprise breakfast
Postman Pat and the frog-pie dinner
Postman Pat and the mushroom tea
Postman Pat and the goat's supper

John Cunliffe
Illustrated by Stuart Trotter

from the original television designs by Ivor Wood

Hodder
Children's
Books

A division of Hodder Headline Limited

Postman Pat™

and the surprise breakfast

Flip-flop went the cat flap.
Out came Jess, to see
what he could find
for his breakfast.

Flip-flop went Pat's slippers on the stairs.
Down came Pat, to see what he could find
for his breakfast.

Sara and Julian stayed in bed. It was half-term,
so they could have an extra snooze.
"Never mind half-term," said Pat, "there are still
letters to deliver."

He switched the kettle on.
He poured some milk for Jess.
He looked in the bread bin.
"Only enough for two slices,"
he said.

He cut the bread carefully and
popped it in the toaster.
His elbow caught the milk bottle.
All the milk was spilt.
Pat ran for the mop to clean it up.
There was a smell of burning!

"Oh, help!"

It was the kettle. Pat had forgotten to fill it with water!
Oh, dear! It was red hot. It blew its fuse!
There would be no tea now.
Pat switched it off and had a drink of water.
There was another smell of burning.

Pat had forgotten the toast.

"Oh, help!"

"It's burnt!" said Pat, throwing it in the bin.
"There'll be no breakfast today, by the looks of it."

In came Jess.
He drank his milk.
Then he brought Pat
a dead mouse.
"Oh, Jess!" said Pat.
"I can't eat a mouse
for my breakfast.
Never mind, we'd
better be on our way."
Off they went.

Pat was very hungry. He saw some blackberries along the hedges and stopped to eat some. "Delicious," said Pat.

They collected the letters from the post office.
"Have a cup of tea and a biscuit," said Mrs Goggins.
"Thanks," said Pat. "Just what I need."

There were some letters for Greendale Farm.
They were up early.
"The cows have to be milked, even if it is half-term,"
said Mrs Pottage. "Would you like some fresh cream
with a scone?"
"I'd love it," said Pat.
Jess had some too.

When Pat arrived at Thompson Ground, Dorothy was just getting a batch of biscuits out of the oven. What a lovely aroma!

"Help yourself," said Dorothy, "the coffee's just ready."
"Grand!" said Pat.

There was a parcel for Miss Hubbard, and she had just made some blackcurrant cordial.
"Here's to your health!" said Miss Hubbard.
"Superb!" said Pat. "I'm feeling better and better."

Ted Glen was making ice-cream. Pat and Jess had a bowl each, with strawberries.

At last it was time for home.

"Whatever happened at breakfast time?"
asked Sara. "I never saw such a mess."
"It was one accident after another,"
said Pat, "*and* we had to rush out
without any breakfast."

"Poor Pat and Jess," said Sara, "you must be starving. Never mind. *We* went shopping, so we can have a really nice dinner."

"We're not exactly starving," said Pat, "but we'll enjoy a good dinner, won't we Jess?"

But Jess wasn't telling any secrets.

Postman Pat™

and the frog-pie dinner

Peter Fogg
Greendale Farm
Greendale

Pat was in a hurry one morning. He had got up late, and he was so late that he had even forgotten what date it was.

So when he met Peter Fogg on his tractor, and Peter said, "Hello, Pat, have you seen any of these flying frogs folks are talking about?" Pat was astonished. He said, "Flying frogs? Is that right? My goodness!"

"Well, keep your eyes skinned," said Peter. "They do say a whole flock flew over the church this morning, and I do believe they're very good to eat."
"Frogs?" said Pat. "Ooooh, I don't fancy eating them, but I would like to see one. What do you think of that, Jess? Flying frogs! What next?"
Jess thought flying mice would be better.

"Tell you what," said Peter, "I'll lend you my fishing net and, if you can catch one, you could ask Sara to make a frog pie."

"Nay, I'd put it in the pond," said Pat. "Thanks, Peter. Cheerio!"

Pat was on his way.
When he called at Greendale Farm, he told Mrs Pottage all about the flying frogs. How she laughed!

"Have you forgotten what day it is?" said Mrs Pottage.
"It's Friday, isn't it?" said Pat.
"No, not the day of the week, the date! It's April the first!"
"Oh," said Pat. "April Fools' Day?"
"Yes, that's right."
"And Peter was just playing a joke on me?"
"That's about it. He caught you out properly, didn't he?"
"He certainly did," said Pat.

Katy and Tom came running in.

"There's a spider on your nose!" said Katy.
"April Fool!" said Pat.
"Oh, he knows," said Tom.

When Pat went home that night, he told Sara and Julian all about Peter's April Fool joke.
"I know what we can do," said Sara. "Peter's bringing a load of logs tomorrow. Let's ask him if he'd like to stay for a spot of dinner. I'll make a mushroom pie, and we'll tell him it's a frog pie!"

"What a good idea," said Pat.
"Then the joke will be on him," said Julian.
"But not an April Fool joke, because that can only be on the first day of April," said Sara.
"And we'll tell him later that it's only mushrooms," said Pat.
"So that he can enjoy his dinner," said Sara.

Sara made a lovely mushroom pie on Saturday morning, and Peter arrived with the logs in good time for dinner.

When they were all unloaded, Pat said,
"We have a special treat for dinner."
"I know," said Peter, "steak and kidney pud.
My favourite!"

"No," said Sara. "It's a special treat. Flying-frog pie."
"What?" said Peter. "Did you say . . . ?"
"Frog pie," said Pat.
"Frog pie?" said Peter. "Well . . . I don't feel very
hungry . . . "

Sara sliced up the mushroom pie.
"Do have a piece," she said. "It's delicious!"
Peter watched them all eating the pie. He still didn't
eat his share.

"Shall we tell him?" said Julian.
"Yes," said Pat.
"It's mushroom pie," said Sara.
"Mushroom?"
"Yes!"
"Oh!" Peter began to laugh. "I love mushroom pie!"

When he had eaten it up, he said, "Well, the joke was on
me! It was a lovely pie!"
"Better than a frog pie?" said Pat.
"Much better," said Peter.

But Jess thought a mouse pie would be best of all.

Postman Pat™

and the mushroom tea

Postman Pat was on his way with the Greendale
post. When he called at Thompson Ground, Sam's
mobile shop was just stopping ahead of him . . .

"Do you like mushrooms?" said Sam.
"I love them," said Pat. "I really do. Could I have half a pound, please?"
"Well, no," said Sam, "you can't."
"Well, what are you on about?" said Pat.

"I haven't got any mushrooms today," said Sam, "but I have these boxes to grow them in."
"Boxes?" said Pat.

"That's it. You just put one of these boxes in your
cellar, or under the stairs – somewhere cool and dark."
"I'm not very good at growing things," said Pat.
"It's easy," said Sam. "Look, it tells you on the lid
what to do. All you have to do is to water it, and pick
the mushrooms when they're ready."
"All right, I'll have a go," said Pat.

He put the mushroom box into his van.
He had a peep inside. There was only
some soil in the bottom. No sign of any
mushrooms. Jess thought it looked like
a good place to hunt for mice.
Pat took his mushroom box home and
put it in the cupboard under the stairs.
He watered the soil inside.
"Now, then, I don't want any mess,"
said Sara.

Julian helped with the watering.
Jess kept an eye on the box,
just in case it grew any mice.
For three days nothing
happened. Nothing
grew at all.

Then, on Thursday,
Sara looked in the box.
She shouted to Pat,
"Quick, come and look
in your mushroom box!"
Pat came running.
"Wow!" he said.
It was full of
mushrooms!

Pat and Julian picked them,
and Sara fried them in butter.
They had them on toast.
"Delicious!" said Sara.
And they were.
"The best I ever tasted,"
said Pat.
Jess didn't like them.

The mushrooms went on
growing and growing.
They filled the box. They
filled it again . . .
and again . . .
and again.

They had them fried, they had them grilled, in pies, in risotto, in omelettes, in soup.

The mushrooms went on growing.

One day, Pat said to the Reverend Timms,
"I'm tired of mushrooms!"
"Tell you what," said the Reverend. "We could have
a Grand Mushroom Tea on the vicarage lawn. That
would use up your mushrooms and we could raise
some money for the church roof."
"What a brilliant idea!" said Pat.

COME
GRAND
EAT

They put a notice in the Pencaster Gazette, and posters in the Pencaster shops. Mrs Goggins, Miss Hubbard, Ted Glen and Pat made mushroom pies, mushroom pizzas, mushroom sandwiches and mushroom soup.

Then, one sunny Saturday, they set out tables and chairs under the trees. Soon, all the tables were full. Everyone said, "What delicious mushrooms!"

There was enough money at the end of the day to mend all the leaks in the church roof, and all the mushrooms had been eaten.

The box stopped growing mushrooms after that.
Sara said, "It's growing something else."

Pat looked inside. It was full of ants! He took
the box to the far end of the garden, and
put it in a corner of the shed.

Pat and Sara and Julian forgot about the mushroom box, but Jess didn't. He kept his eye on it for a long time. One dark night, he heard a scuffling sound in the box. The lid pushed open and out popped two mice.

"That's better," thought Jess. "Much better."

Postman Pat ™

and the goat's supper

One morning, Pat had a parcel for Miss Hubbard.
It was a big, soft, squashy parcel.
"I wonder what it is?" said Pat to Jess. "It feels like
a cushion."

Miss Hubbard was pleased to see her parcel.
"Have a cup of coffee," she said, "while I open it."

It wasn't a cushion at all.
It was a blue jumper.
She tried it on.
"Lovely," she said,
"just the thing for wearing
on my bike on chilly days.
It's from Cousin Nellie,
in Nelson."

"What a kind cousin," said Pat. "Does she knit things for men?"
"I don't think so," said Miss Hubbard.
"Pity," said Pat. "Well, thanks for the coffee. I'll be on my way now. Bye!"

Pat saw the blue jumper again, one evening, when
he was going home after choir practice. It was
hanging on Miss Hubbard's washing line.
"She's gone to bed and forgotten it," said Pat. "But
it'll be all right. There's no wind to blow it away."

There was no wind, but there was a hungry goat. No one saw it jump over the wall, looking for something to eat for its supper. Its bright eyes spotted the jumper, and it trotted over to see what it was.

Then it did what some goats will do. It tugged and it nibbled . . .

and chewed at it . . .

and ate a great chunk
out of the sleeve. Oh,
what a mischief that goat was!

It went all about Miss Hubbard's garden, nibbling at this and that – flowers of all sorts, lettuce, a cabbage leaf – and poking its nose everywhere.

It knocked a bucket over, and gave Miss Hubbard a dreadful fright.

Worst of all was when she got up next morning and saw the hole in the hedge, and then saw the hole in her new jumper!

"Oh, my jumper," wailed Miss Hubbard. "It was my favourite."

When Pat came, he said, "Don't you worry. Just write to Cousin Nellie. She'll be able to knit a new sleeve, in no time at all."

Before the end of the week, there was a postcard
from Nellie.
"It's not good news," said Pat, as he gave the card
to Miss Hubbard. "She says that she has no more
wool of that colour."
"Oh, deary me, it's just what I feared."
"Don't take on," said Pat. "I'll keep a look out.
There must be some of it somewhere."

ss R. Hubbard
thlands Farm Cottage
ndale
t Britain

Pat tied a strand of the wool on his steering wheel, to remind him. One day, he called on Granny Dryden and, there she was, knitting a scarf for Ted Glen: a blue scarf.

"The very same colour!" said Pat, running to get
the wool from his van. It was a perfect match.
"Can you knit sleeves?" said Pat.
"I was knitting sleeves before you were born," said
Granny Dryden.

Pat told her all about Miss Hubbard and her jumper.
"Sounds like one of Alf's goats," said Granny Dryden.
"I have a lot of that colour. I was wondering what to do
with it."

Granny Dryden knitted a new sleeve, and Miss Hubbard said her mended jumper was like new. Never again did she leave it out to dry at night.

As for Alf's goat . . . Alf mended the hole in the fence, and it had to make do with oats and grass for its supper after that!

More Postman Pat adventures:

Postman Pat and the mystery tour
Postman Pat and the beast of greendale
Postman Pat and the robot
Postman Pat takes flight
Postman Pat and the big surprise
Postman Pat paints the ceiling
Postman Pat has too many parcels
Postman Pat and the suit of armour
Postman Pat and the hole in the road
Postman Pat has the best village
Postman Pat misses the show
Postman Pat follows a trail
Postman Pat in a muddle